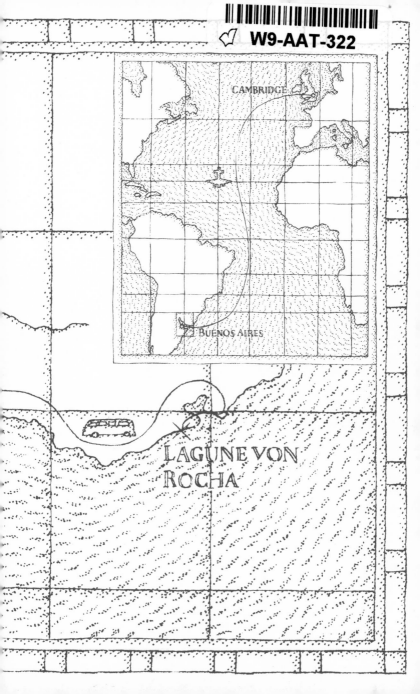

CAMBRIDGE

BUENOS AIRES

LAGUNE VON
ROCHA

the house of paper

Carlos María Domínguez

the house of paper

Illustrations by Peter Sís

———

Translated from the Spanish by
Nick Caistor

HARCOURT, INC.

Orlando   Austin   New York   San Diego   Toronto   London www.HarcourtBooks.com

Library of Congress Cataloging-in-Publication Data
Domínguez, Carlos María, 1955–
[Casa de papel. English]
The house of paper/Carlos María Domínguez; illustrated by Peter Sís;
translated from the Spanish by Nick Caistor.

p.   cm.
I. Sís, Peter, 1949–   II. Caistor, Nick.   III. Title.
PQ7798.14.O385C3713   2004
863'.64—dc22   2005002401
ISBN-13: 978-0-15-101147-6
ISBN-10: 0-15-101147-8

This is a translation of *La casa de papel.*

Text set in Legacy Serif Book
Designed by Linda Lockowitz

Printed in the United States of America

First U.S. edition
A C E G I K J H F D B

In memory of the great Joseph

the house of paper

one

One day in the spring of 1998, Bluma Lennon bought a secondhand copy of Emily Dickinson's poems in a bookshop in Soho, and as she reached the second poem on the first street corner, she was knocked down by a car.

Books change people's destinies. Some have read *The Tiger of Malaysia* and become professors of literature in remote universities. *Demian* converted tens of thousands of young men to Eastern philosophy, Hemingway made sportsmen of them, Alexandre Dumas complicated the lives of thousands of women, quite a few of whom were saved from suicide by cookbooks. Bluma was their victim.

But not the only one. An elderly professor of classical languages, Leonard Wood, was left paralyzed after being struck on the head by five volumes of the *Encyclopaedia Britannica* that fell from a shelf in his library; my friend Richard broke a leg when he tried to reach William Faulkner's *Absalom, Absalom!,* which was so awkwardly placed he fell off his stepladder. Another of my friends in Buenos Aires caught TB in the basement of a public archive, and I even knew a dog from Chile that died of indigestion from swallowing the pages of *The Brothers Karamazov* one afternoon when rage got the better of him.

Whenever my grandmother saw me reading in bed, she would say: "Stop that, books are dangerous." For many years I thought she was simply ignorant, but the passage of time has shown just how sensible my German grandmother was.

Many of the most important people in Cambridge were present for Bluma's funeral. At the service, Professor Robert Laurel made a splendid farewell speech, later published as a pamphlet on

2

account of its academic merit. He touched on Bluma's brilliant university career, the sensibility and intelligence that had characterized her forty-five years. In the main part of his eulogy he mentioned the decisive contribution she had made to the investigation of Anglo-Saxon influences in Latin American literature. But he ended with a sentence that caused great controversy: "Bluma devoted her life to literature, never dreaming it would take her from this world."

Those who accused Laurel of ruining his speech with this "clumsy euphemism" were opposed by the steadfast defense of his assistants. A few days later, at my friend Ann's house, I heard John Bernon insisting to a group of Laurel's disciples:

"She was killed by a car, not by a poem."

"Nothing exists beyond its representation," argued two young men and a Jewish girl, who was the most outspoken of the three. "Everyone has the right to choose the representation they wish."

"And to produce bad literature. All right," retorted the elderly gentleman with the air of false

conciliation that had given him the reputation in the university of being a cynic, "so there are a million car bumpers loose on the streets of the city which can show you just what a good noun is capable of."

Arguments about the infamous phrase spread throughout the university. There was even a student competition on the theme "Relations between reality and language." The number of steps Bluma took on the Soho pavement were calculated, as were the verses of the poems she had managed to read, and the speed of the car. There was furious debate about the semiotics of London traffic, and the cultural, urban, and linguistic context of the second in which literature and the world imploded on the body of our dear Bluma. I had to take over from her in the Department of Hispanic Studies, use her office and teach her courses, so I was far from impressed by the direction the arguments were taking.

One morning I received a package addressed to my deceased colleague. The stamps were Uruguayan, and but for the lack of a sender's address, I would have thought it was one of those books she was often sent by authors in the hope she would review it for an academic publication. Bluma never did so unless the author was sufficiently well-known for her to derive something from it. She would usually ask me to take them down to the reserve collection, after scrawling "UTC" (Unlikely To Consult) on them, which more or less condemned the works to oblivion.

It was indeed a book, but not of the kind I had been expecting. No sooner had I opened the package than I felt an instinctive nervousness. I went to the office door, closed it, and returned to the broken-spined old copy of *The Shadow-Line*. I was aware of the thesis Bluma was writing on Joseph Conrad. But the extraordinary thing was that there was a filthy crust on its front and back covers. There was a film of cement particles on the page edges that left a fine dust on the surface of the polished desk.

I took out a handkerchief and to my astonishment picked up a small piece of grit. There was no doubt it was Portland cement, the remains of a mortar that must have been stuck more firmly to the book before someone had made a determined attempt to remove it.

There was no missive inside, only the battered book I could not bring myself to pick up. When I lifted the cover carefully with my fingers, I found a dedication from Bluma. It was written in green ink, and was definitely in her handwriting, neat and round like everything of hers. It was not hard to decipher: "For Carlos, this novel that has accompanied me from airport to airport, in memory of those crazy days in Monterrey. Sorry for being a bit of a witch and as I told you right from the start: you'll never do anything that will surprise me. 8 June 1996."

I knew Bluma's flat, the dietary food she kept in the fridge, the smell of her sheets, the perfume of her underwear. I shared her bed with two deputy heads of departments and a student who had somehow got onto the list. And like all the others, I knew about her trip to a congress in Monterrey, where she had one of those lightning romances she offered herself to satisfy her vanity, threatened as it was by the loss of her youth, her two husbands, and the dream of traveling up the River Macondo in a canoe (an obsession she had inherited from reading *One Hundred Years of Solitude*). So why was the book being returned to Cambridge after two years? Where had it been? And what was Bluma meant to read into the traces of cement?

I have held in my hands the marvelous *Irish Fairy and Folk Tales,* with a prologue by William Butler Yeats and original illustrations by James Torrance, as well as the *Correspondance inédite du Marquis de Sade et de ses proches et de ses familiers,* I have been lucky enough to hold some incunables for a few short minutes, open their pages, feel their weight and that sense of solitary privilege, but no other book has affected me so much as that paperback, whose damp, warped pages seemed to be calling out to me.

I put it back in the bag, slipped it into my brief-case, then wiped the dust from the desk as stealthily as a thief.

Over the next week I looked through Bluma's archives to try to find the names and addresses usually given out at congresses of critics and writers. I found the list in an ocher-colored folder with "Memories of Monterrey" written on the cover. Neither of the two writers who attended from Uruguay was called Carlos, but I noted down their addresses and e-mails anyway. I told myself I should not get mixed up in Bluma's private life, but at the same time I felt that such an odd book—illegible beyond any message she was meant to read in the cement—deserved to be returned to whoever had sent it.

I put the book on the lectern of a table in my study, and must confess that for several nights I stared at it with a mixture of curiosity and anxiety. Perhaps because Alice's vacuum cleaner left no trace of dust on even the highest shelves of my library, and certainly not on the carpet or any of the tables, the paperback upset the balance of the room like a tramp at an imperial feast. It had been published by Emecé in Buenos Aires, and printed in November 1946. With some effort I discovered it was part of the "Ivory Gate" collection edited by Borges and Bioy Casares. Underneath the lime or cement, there was the faint outline of a boat, and what looked like several fishes, although I could not be certain.

Over the following days, Alice put a duster under the lectern to prevent the dust spoiling the glass tabletop, and changed it each morning with that quiet discretion of hers which had won me over ever since she first came to work for me.

The first e-mail replies from the city of Nuevo Léon in Mexico were disappointing. They consisted of the list of participants I already had, the congress program, and a map of the city. However, one of the Uruguayan writers told me that someone called Carlos Brauer had also attended the conference. Brauer was a bibliophile from Uruguay, and the writer had seen him leave one of the dinners with Bluma on his arm, both of them the worse for wear after drinking several tequilas and dancing some incredible Colombian *vallenatos*. "Please treat this in confidence," he wrote, "because I'm being indiscreet."

I imagined Bluma dancing by candlelight in a colonial patio, one typically hot, stormy Mexican night, determined to prove that though she might not be Latin, she could dance all the same, that she was serious but not ridiculous, and was sensual in her own way. Then I saw her stumbling down a cobbled street, holding hands with the man leading her on—happily perhaps?—as their shadows disappeared in dark doorways.

The writer also told me that Brauer had moved to Rocha, a department of Uruguay on the Atlantic Ocean, and that he had lost contact with him, but if I gave him a few days, he could find out how to get in touch with a friend of his.

Fifteen years is a long time, and that was how long I had been in England. Every three years, I went back to Buenos Aires to visit my mother, renew links with friends from the past, and immerse myself in the language spoken by the varied fauna of Buenos Aires, and yet I hardly knew Uruguay. I have a dim memory of crossing to Montevideo by night ferry when I was five and my father carrying me off the boat. On that

11

occasion, a friend had invited me to spend a few days in Punta del Este, but I had never been to Rocha. I had only a vague idea of where it was.

The southern beaches of Uruguay did not give me the impression of a dirty windscreen on a rainy day. Perhaps it was the immensity of the sky, the wilderness of sand and wind, added to Carlos Brauer's story, which in my mind linked the coast of Rocha with windscreens and the panic I feel whenever someone praises all the books I possess. Every year I give away at least fifty of them to my students, yet I still cannot avoid putting in another double row of shelves; the books are advancing silently, innocently through my house. There is no way I can stop them.

I have often asked myself why I keep books that could only ever be of any use in a distant future, titles remote from my usual concerns, those I have read once and will not open again for many years, if ever! But how could I throw away *The Call of the Wild*, for example, without destroying one of the building bricks of my childhood, or *Zorba the Greek*,

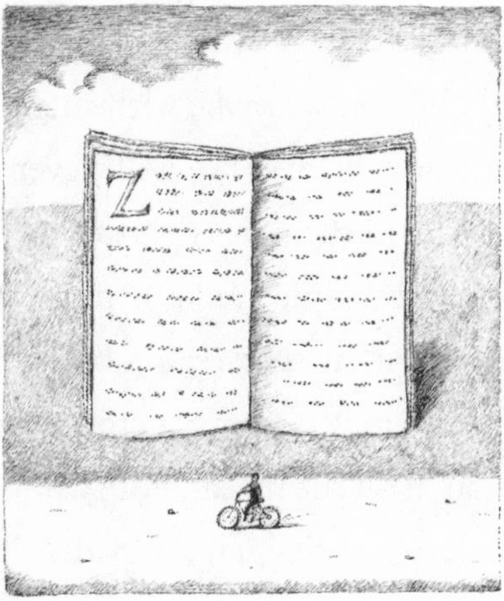

which brought my adolescence to a tear-stained end, *The Twenty-Fifth Hour* and all those other volumes consigned to the topmost shelves, where they lie untouched and silent in that sacred trust of which we are so proud.

It is often much harder to get rid of books than it is to acquire them. They stick to us in that pact of need and oblivion we make with them, witnesses to a moment in our lives we will never see again. While they are still there, it is part of us. I have noticed that many people make a note of the day, month, and year that they read a book; they build up a secret calendar. Others, before lending one, write their name on the flyleaf, note whom they lent it to in an address book, and add the date. I have known some book owners who stamp them or slip a card between their pages the way they do in public libraries. Nobody wants to mislay a book. We prefer to lose a ring, a watch, our umbrella, rather than a book whose pages we will never read again, but which retains, just in the sound of its title, a remote and perhaps long-lost emotion.

The truth is that in the end, the size of a library does matter. We lay the books out for inspection like a huge exposed brain, offering miserable excuses and feigned modesty. I once knew a professor of classical languages who deliberately took his time preparing the coffee in his kitchen so that his visitor could admire the titles on his shelves. When he could tell the effect had been achieved, he would appear in the room with the tray and a broad smile.

As readers, we spy on our friends' libraries, if only as a pastime. Occasionally we hope to find a book we want to read but do not have, or to find out what the animal opposite us has devoured. And at home, we leave a colleague sitting in the living room, and return to find him standing there, without fail, sniffing at our books.

There is a moment, however, when we have accumulated so many books that they cross an invisible line, and what was once a sense of pride becomes a burden, because from now on space will always be a problem. The day the copy of *The Shadow-Line* came into my hands, I had been worrying about where I could possibly fit in a new set of shelves. From that moment on, it became an ever-present warning for me.

By now, however, it was exam time, and this took my mind off the book. It lay there on my lectern while I dealt with my own classes and Bluma's. I was overwhelmed by mounds of essays and practical work. Soon, though, the summer vacation arrived, and I decided to bring forward the visit to my mother, at the same time giving myself the satisfaction of returning the book and informing the man, who at that moment meant nothing to me, of Bluma's unfortunate end. There is no denying I also wanted to know his secret.

two

A week later and I was in Buenos Aires. I found the city full of glass, a lot more modern; I found my mother and friends more despondent, as though the deafening roar of the traffic, the lights, the televisions in the bars, needed the depression of the inhabitants to fill the lungs of the city with the air needed to help it grow.

Avenida Santa Fe had replaced Avenida Corrientes as the main point of interest. The avenue was full of big, posh bookshops, megastores selling CDs, audio equipment, books, smart cafés, cinemas and theaters, outside which stood lines of supplicant beggars.

People in the city walked with cell phones to

their ears; they drove with the gadget wedged against one shoulder; they talked into them on buses, in supermarkets, even while they were sweeping the pavements, as if they had all succumbed to an oral fever.

One afternoon I went for a walk in the port. This was something I did regularly when I was living in Buenos Aires, strolling among great coils of rope, open brick warehouses, cranes, ships, seamen, and gulls. Now, on each visit I performed the same rite, as if returning to the pages of a book from childhood that preserved a certain period, as well as being the entrance and exit to the city. This time what I discovered were luxury restaurants, lofts, cafés, and doormen from a world so completely transformed, so unremittingly on display, and so grotesquely expensive that I felt cast out of it like a stone.

That same afternoon on the underground I saw a young girl with an accordion on her lap. For a few seconds I thought from her sad expression and shabby clothes that she must have come from one of the provinces of the interior: Corrientes, Tucumán, or

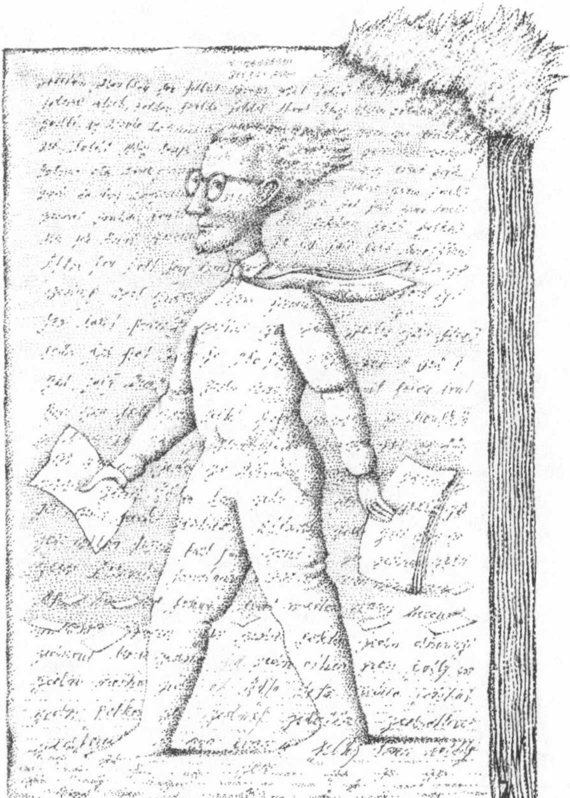

Misiones, following in the wake of other waifs and strays. She must have noticed my interest, because she stared at me and began to play a gypsy tune that made me change my mind. She finished playing when the train reached the next station, and got out. I do not know why, but I felt like following her. There was something so sorrowful about her, so sweet and dreadful at the same time, just like the corner of the port now lost to me forever. But the doors closed in my face. I was later told she was one of the Kosovars who went around Buenos Aires on the buses and trains, the children playing accordions while their fathers or mothers begged for money. This banal, definitive explanation seemed to destroy all possibility of astonishment in a way that robbed it of meaning. Buenos Aires has always found a way to surprise me, but now something sordid clung to it even more firmly than the cement on the covers of my book.

Some friends gave me the volumes they had just published, but said little about them. They talked about whether Piglia or Saer had a strategy to place themselves within the corpus of Argentine literature, if it was a good idea to say you would take part and then not turn up to a roundtable or a book launch, whether you should "aim for" academic critics or newspaper ones, go into hiding, choose small publishing houses that would take great care over your book or be a celebrity for a month with a Spanish publisher, then vanish like a shooting star from the new titles table.

Their literary aspirations amounted to a political campaign, or perhaps more precisely a military strategy to find a way to demolish the walls of anonymity, an insuperable barrier only a privileged few managed to scale. There were brilliant stars in the literary firmament, people who earned a fortune overnight with dreadful books that were promoted by their publishers, in newspaper supplements, through marketing campaigns, literary prizes, ghastly films, and prominent, paid-for positions in bookshop windows. They talked of this in bars as if it were a chaotic battlefield a writer had to traverse not during the adventure of writing—

although some did start then—but as soon as that was over. The publishers complained of a lack of good books, of the writers of the "horseshit" brought out by the big publishers, and everyone had an indignant demand, a justification for their failure, a desperate ambition. In Buenos Aires, books had become the center of a nightmarish strategic war, talent a question of ubiquity and power.

A week later I took the hydrofoil across the River Plate to the unknown shore. The river was dun-colored and quiet, and as I left Buenos Aires behind I could feel myself recovering a sense of proportion in the expanse of water and broad horizon that made it easier to breathe, to discover some space inside me.

The arrival at the port of Montevideo was un-dramatic and soothing. The city pushed out into the river with a reckless determination that made its few tall buildings look like cranes, like those of a big beached fishing boat, while its bay, crowned in the distance by a low hill, gave off a feeling of maternal seclusion.

A few hours later I went into a shop in the old

town, where I was to meet Jorge Dinarli, one of the best secondhand dealers in Montevideo. An employee led me through a large colonial-style room to a dark office lined with books that lay beyond the circle of light provided by a weak lamp tilted over a green writing pad. I was received by a man with graying hair who spoke in an extremely low voice, whose name had been given me by the writer who had traveled to Monterrey.

He had indeed known Brauer for many years, although only in a professional capacity, as he had other bibliophiles in the city.

"There are two sorts, if I may explain: on the one hand, the collectors, whose aim is to amass rare editions: Horacio Quiroga's magazine in Salto, not only the books written by Borges, but all his articles; editions by Colombo, Güiraldes's editor, or the exquisite bindings signed by Bonet, even though they never even open them except to look at the pages, in the same way for example, that people contemplate a beautiful object, a rare piece. On the other, there are bibliophiles who are readers, who throughout their life have built up important libraries. I would include Brauer among this group. Book lovers, capable of spending a considerable amount of money for a volume with which they will spend many hours, concerned only to study and understand.

"Perhaps I'm not the right person to talk to you about Brauer. There are others who were closer to him, who knew him well, and will be able to tell you what happened, especially Agustín Delgado. I'll give you his phone number. I can only give you the general picture."

When Dinarli said "what happened," he lowered his gaze, suddenly ill at ease. Was he referring to Brauer's move to Rocha? Was there something else? I opened my briefcase, took out the package, and put the book on his desk.

He stared intently at it, and sat motionless for several seconds, as if reluctant to touch it.

"I came here to give him back this book," I said, keen to see what impression my words had on him. He bent forward and peered at the volume.

"Where did you get it?"

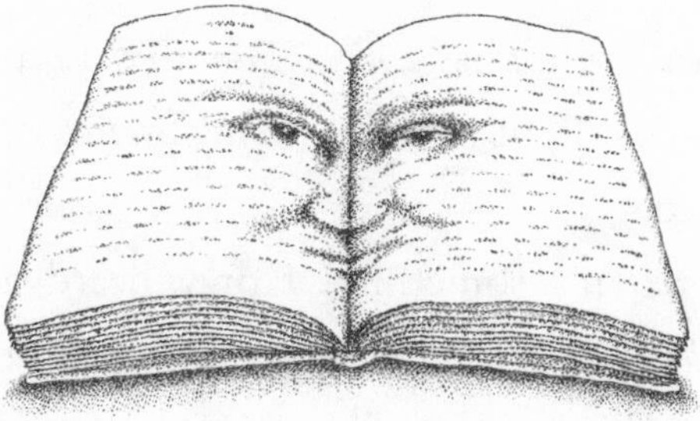

"It arrived in my office at the University of Cambridge. Addressed to a colleague, not to me. But it came too late, so I decided to give it back."

"I don't know if that will be possible."

"Is Rocha a long way away?"

"It's not the town of Rocha. He lived near La Paloma, but I don't think he's there anymore."

"Why?"

"Please, put that away," Dinarli said, pointing to the book. I put it back into my briefcase, doubly intrigued.

"Look, it's something I only heard about. I wouldn't like to say anything about it. You should talk to Delgado. He'll tell you. You need to call him after ten at night or early in the morning. I'll give you his number. Don't worry. You are in possession of something with an unfortunate history. You'll understand why soon enough. I don't know what you'll do with it. I've no idea what I would do with a book like that. Don't take offense. We love books here," he added, pointing to his bookcases. "You really ought to talk to Delgado."

He opened his address book and wrote down a number on the back of one of his business cards.

"I can only tell you trivial things. I met Brauer some years ago at an auction, because he had teamed up with old man Martel. I know that he used to work in the Foreign Ministry, and that if Martel did not lift his pencil to bid when a lot of books was being sold, either Brauer or Delgado would buy it. Usually American literature. But they would always have to wait for the old man to decide, and he had an infallible nose for a bargain. Martel took Brauer under his wing somewhat at the start, passing on what he wasn't particularly interested in. As you know, there can be anything in a lot of books. Worthless editions together with real jewels. Books printed in editions of three hundred or five hundred, which have become very hard to find and are therefore very expensive. People once thought printed books would mean an end to all that. A machine could produce thousands, hundreds of thousands of copies. Now look. Time does its work. Time and the stupidity of binders nowadays, who guillotine old books to even them up, for example, without realizing they are slicing off hundreds of dollars, chopping up a ruby, knocking feathers off the Victory of Samothrace, if you'll pardon my indignation. I can't persuade them to give up the obscure pleasure of the guillotine."

Dinarli recovered his composure, and fell back into the whisper with which he had greeted me. The topic made him uneasy, and he did not seem sure exactly whom he was talking to.

"Brauer collected literature," he went on, "especially Spanish first editions, art books, the nineteenth-century novel, French and Russian in particular. That was his field. He once bought some pamphlets by the Carreras brothers from me, the ones Neruda was interested in. If you remember, Neruda used to come to Montevideo in order to . . ."

"He had a lover, in Atlántida I think," I helped him.

"Well, he would call in here, and was always interested in the Carreras brothers' pamphlets, which they printed on the move while the Chilean revolution raged around them. And then Brauer once offered me a set of Martín Fierro magazines, because he had two. We got on well. There's no doubt he was a scholar. The magazines had writing in the margins, they were full of commentaries and annotations—rather untidily written, I must say. But that just shows Brauer was an old-style reader in the mold of Martel, Horacio Arredondo, or Simón Lucuix, rather than a collector. At least, he used to be.

"I know he lived in a large house on Calle Cuareim, though I've never been there. Before he moved, before he took that unbelievable decision, we had been discussing his Mexican collection. Don't worry. His friend Delgado will tell you everything. Look, we could have bought his library. I know it was very important, and with the passage of time I learned it contained some very rare books, although as I said I never got to see them. I heard, for example, that he had complete books by León Pallièrè and Vidal, with the engravings still intact, and they alone are worth around twenty thousand dollars nowadays. But when something extraordinary happens, people invent stories about it, so it becomes impossible to distinguish what is true from what is fantasy. The best thing is if you talk to Delgado, although to be frank I'm not sure you'll be able to return the book. I don't think anyone knows what's become of Brauer. Now I hope you won't mind if I say you shouldn't waste any more time here."

Dinarli stood up, and I could see he was unsteady on his feet as he came round the desk toward me.

"If you'll allow me to say so," he whispered, "If I were you, I'd be very careful when you show that book to Delgado. As you'll find out soon enough, he's a rather special person."

He accompanied me to his office door, handed me his card and wished me luck.

Back in my hotel, my initial sense of bewilderment had eased, and I realized *The Shadow-Line* had led me to a region of rarefied waters. I wandered around this unobtrusively dirty, unobtrusively old city, where even its inhabitants seemed to live un-obtrusive lives. I was struck by the slow-moving buses, and by how friendly were the waiters in bars, hotel employees, and taxi drivers, as if a time that had come to a musty halt were concealing a dense web of secrets beneath its air of mild reticence.

It may have been that I was under the spell of a sentence in the author's note to *The Shadow-Line*, which I was finding impossible to hand back, and which was becoming more disturbing with each passing hour. Conrad had never visited Monte-video on his travels, but in order to deny any super-natural element in his work, he wrote: "The world of the living contains enough marvels and myster-ies as it is—marvels and mysteries acting upon our emotions and intelligence in ways so inexplicable that it would almost justify the conception of life as an enchanted state."

I could not get this out of my mind as I mulled over what Dinarli had said to me, the strong im-pression his office had made on me, or the gigantic bow of a boat glimpsed at the far end of a street thronged with traffic, bank clerks, and newspaper kiosks. All these elements were flung together in a random fashion: the ship's red bow and the gray city were like two worlds embedded in each other, with the result that both of them seemed unreal.

three

I called Delgado at eleven o'clock that evening. He sounded surprised, but agreed to see me the next afternoon and gave me his address, in a neighborhood called Punta Carretas, or "Cart Point," a juxtaposition I found hard to reconcile.

Delgado had spoken of "his study," but as soon as I discovered the modern building and reached the fifth floor, where he was waiting for me, I realized I had got completely the wrong impression. Delgado was tall and thin, and wore a blue suit with a black tie. He showed me into a large living room whose beveled windows looked out onto the street. He observed my astonishment with pride. The walls were crammed with enormous glass bookcases that stretched from floor to ceiling. And not just in this room, but in the next one too. He showed me around the whole apartment, and everywhere I discovered the same cases stuffed with books, and in the corridors, carousels where large dictionaries were kept, vinyl records were overflowing from wardrobes, and books were all over the bathroom, in the maid's room, the kitchen, the back rooms. I guessed that he did not actually live here, and when we were seated in two armchairs in the main living room, next to his sound system, he confirmed this.

"I live on the floor above," he explained, "with my wife and, until recently, my son. I used to think it would be good to build an interior staircase between the two floors, but before it was too late I realized that books should not get contaminated by domestic life. They would be bound to get dirty."

He had crossed his legs, and between the top of his sock and the trouser turnup I could see a few inches of delicate white skin—something that had he been aware of, I was sure he would have been at pains to conceal. His freshly shaved face, neat hair with flecks of gray, and his generally well-groomed appearance warned me I should tread warily.

"How many books do you have?" I asked.

"To tell you the truth, I've given up counting. But I think there must be around eighteen thousand. I've been buying books here and there ever since I can remember. To build up a library is to create a life. It's never just a random collection of books."

"I don't quite understand," I said.

"You go on adding them to the shelves, and they seem to constitute a collection, but I would say that's an illusion. We pursue some topics, and at the end of a certain length of time we find ourselves defining worlds, or if you prefer, we are tracing the steps of a journey, the advantage being that we can conserve its traces. It's not a simple matter. It's a process by which we complete bibliographies: we start with a reference to a book we don't have, then when we have acquired that one, it leads us on to another. Although I have to confess my own reading is very limited. I need to consult all the notes that accompany a book, and to understand the meaning of every concept, so it's hard for me to sit down and read one book without another twenty alongside it, sometimes merely to interpret a single chapter fully. Of course, it's something that fascinates me."

He smiled a conspiratorial smile I willingly shared.

"But unfortunately," he went on, "how many hours a day can I devote to reading? At most four or five. I work from eight o'clock to five in a position of some responsibility. But all the time I'm longing to be back here. In my cave, if you'll pardon the expression, where I can spend a few happy hours until ten o'clock, when I usually go upstairs for supper."

"I'm not interested in first editions. What I want is to have the book within reach in the best possible condition, otherwise I become anxious. These cases you can see are made from lapacho, a wood that has no cracks that insects can penetrate; I ordered the shelves especially: they are ten hardwood boards stuck together with an insect-repellent glue, and I put glass fronts on them because books obviously accumulate dust. From time to time, though, I have them fumigated just in case, because you can never be too sure. Silverfish drove Brauer mad."

"Did he keep his books in glass cases?" I asked, sniffing my opportunity.

He smiled and said nothing for a few moments.

"He kept them however he could, because he didn't have the means to conserve his amazing collection properly. I often argued with him about it. Brauer was a compulsive reader. Whatever money he had, he spent on books. Ever since I met him years ago at the book stalls in Tristán Narvaja, I realized he was incurable. You can tell it by the parchmentlike skin book addicts have."

I lowered my eyes to the bare patch of his leg. It was dry and yellowish, just like a parchment. Delgado caught my gaze, and immediately adjusted his trouser leg.

"He had a fairly important job in the Foreign Ministry," he continued. "He lived alone in a house

on Calle Cuareim and devoured every book he could lay his hands on, as well as endless packets of pastilles and sweets that littered his floor. His habit of eating sweets replaced cigarettes, which the doctors had forbidden him, and was as all-consuming as his passion for books, which he kept in vast bookcases that filled the rooms end to end and from floor to ceiling. Not only that, they were piled up in the kitchen, the bathroom, and in his bedroom as well. Not his original bedroom, because he had been forced out of there, but in the attic where he had taken refuge, next to another little bathroom. The stairs leading up to the attic were also full of books, and it was nineteenth-century French literature which watched over his scant hours of sleep.

"He had complete collections of old magazines, a lot of classical history, almost the whole of nineteenth-century Russian literature, collections of American literature, art books, philosophical essays and commentaries on them; the entire Greek and Elizabethan theater, Peruvian poetry up to the middle of the twentieth century, several Mexican incunables, first editions of Arlt, Borges, Vallejo, Onetti, and Valle Inclán, not to mention all the encyclopaedias, dictionaries, pamphlets, and books by River Plate travelers he owned also.

"In the end he possessed so many volumes—more than twenty thousand I believe—that his fairly substantial living room was filled with the kind of stacks you see in public libraries. His bathroom had books on every wall, except where the shower was, and they only avoided being ruined because he had given up hot showers to prevent any steam. Summer or winter, he always took cold showers."

Delgado stroked the nape of his neck and smiled without looking at me.

"Do you know what he did?" he asked, his eyes on my face once more. "He gave his car to a friend so that he could fill his garage with books. He didn't do very well out of the exchange. The next winter was terrible, and the leaks got at his collection of *Summa Artis,* which has a very thin, satin paper. It was completely ruined. I had two sets, so I gave him one as a replacement."

"I presume he was comfortably off," I managed to slip in.

"He was fortunate enough to retire young and to have inherited from his mother. In fact, we had lengthy arguments about how that money should be used. I insisted he shouldn't waste it buying more books at auction, but should conserve his library. But as I've already told you, he was a voracious reader who spent not just four hours but most of the day and night with his books. And of course, he wrote comments on all of them. I prefer not to mark books. I make my notes elsewhere, and slot them into the pages they refer to while I'm working on a book. When I've finished, I take them out and throw them in the wastepaper basket."

"Why don't you keep them?" I asked in astonishment.

"Well, not everyone can write. I mean, not everyone should write. I make a note of whatever interests me. Associations. Pointers to other books, a reflection here and there. A reader's notes. For example: the form of this metaphor in Quevedo can be compared to another by Ben-Quzmán, in the anthology of Andalusian Arabic (see the Gredos edition), and the figure of birds that it involves links to the symbology of birds in Lope de Vega's work (consult: collection by the Spanish Higher Council for Scientific Research). Who else would be interested in anything like that?

"I must confess that I've been tempted to publish some of my reflections, but a reader is a traveler through a ready-made landscape. And an infinite one at that. The tree has been written, as has the stone, the wind in its branches, the nostalgia for those branches, and the love to which they lent their shade. For me the greatest joy is to be able to submerge myself for a few hours every day in a human time that otherwise would be alien to me. A lifetime is not enough. If I may purloin half of a sentence by Borges: 'a library is a door in time.'

"Brauer and I often talked about these things. I begged him not to ruin valuable editions with his horrid scribbles. Of course, he never listened to me. I called him insensitive, and he said I was a hypocrite, though naturally neither of us took offense. His defense was that if he wrote in the margins and underlined words, often in different coded colors, he could seize the meaning better. I don't think he would be upset if I repeat one of his expressions, even though it is rather vulgar: 'I fuck with every book, and if I don't leave a mark, there's no orgasm.' To me, any scrawl on a book seems as shocking as his boast. I get tremendous enjoyment from opening a book anywhere and not finding pages dog-eared, from studying a well-judged interlineation, wide white margins; opening an uncut volume on my birthday."

Delgado paused, as if he had just made a rash confession. But he thought twice, and began again:

"None of that mattered to Brauer, with his cannibal pride, his ever-increasing voracity."

He broke off again, with a bitter gesture. He disguised it by standing up. He apologized for not having offered me anything to drink, and went over to a small electric coffee machine.

"You were saying that silverfish drove him mad," I said, as he took two china cups from a small bar.

He raised an eyebrow and finished preparing the coffee.

"There were hundreds, perhaps thousands of them infesting his bookshelves. For a while he kept them under control with fumigations every six months or year. They had begun to ruin important works. He controlled them but never got rid of them altogether. He used unvarnished wood, had a maid who was no longer young, but whom he hadn't the heart to get rid of, who had long since given up trying to reach the corners where moths nested. Above all though, to be honest, he simply had too many books in that house. He would have needed a fortune to protect them from damp, silverfish, moths, dust, spiders. His ambition had somehow grown out of control. I complain about having so little time to read, but just imagine a man who has all day and, if he feels like it, the night too. And money to buy every book he wants. There are no limits. He is at the mercy of his passion. And what is it that passion most wants? If you'll allow me an observation . . . it wants to discover its limit. But that's no easy matter. Brauer was a conqueror more than a traveler. That's what he became. For example: he lost all sense of shame at auctions. And this cost him his friends. Several of his colleagues were hurt when they lost out on lots of books for which they had been waiting a long time, because Brauer bid for them and they couldn't go any higher.

"But that wasn't all. There came a time when even his money was beginning to run out. He wasn't a millionaire. You might say he finally found a limit to his passion. He stopped bidding against people at auctions, and finally stopped going to them altogether. There was a further complication. After many years, his ex-wife demanded money from him through a lawyer, and he found himself faced with the need to sell his house and move."

"You didn't mention he had been married."

"He never talked about it. It had been a long time before I met him, and on the rare occasions we touched on the topic he never told me any details."

Delgado paused while he passed me my coffee cup, and cast me a sideways glance.

"I haven't even asked what brought you here. It was enough for me to know Dinarli had sent you ... You must understand, though, that Brauer was not going to harp on about something that must have been so painful for him."

He had found a way to broach the subject of my being there. But I delayed my reply with a sense of perverse pleasure I cannot explain. We had been talking for some time, but there was still no suggestion of any reason that would justify sending the copy of *The Shadow-Line* to Bluma's office. Yet I could sense we were drawing imperceptibly closer, just as the barque *Otago* in Conrad's novel drifts on despite the ocean's dark calm.

"We didn't say much about another topic either," Delgado said, accepting my reluctance to speak although he was not happy about it. "Whatever the reason, it was clear he had reached a point of no return. He felt trapped by his books. How could he move all those shelves? How could he avoid having to relinquish them? He had devoted his whole life to them. They were his life's work. But apart from the use we few friends made of his library, and some nearby mothers who every so often sent their children to consult a book in order to improve an essay they had to do for school or university, Brauer's life's work was turning into a nightmare.

"What was he to do? If he decided to dispose of his library, he could have offered it to the City, the Ministry, or the Faculty of Humanities. The Uruguayan state has bought many important libraries and established a rich heritage. But I'm ashamed to say that many of those libraries have been looted in the most unbelievable way. People have come to steal the most valuable works. A great Argentine bibliophile sent someone to steal a printed version of *El Misionero*—any works printed in the Jesuit missions are extremely rare, but there was one in the National Library. It was stolen and taken to this gentleman, whose name need not concern us. Years later, his books were sold to the National Library in Lima, and that was where the volume ended up.

"All of which meant that Brauer must have been afraid his books could meet the same fate. In the Faculty of Humanities, important documents from Horacio Arredondo's library were stolen, and others went astray. He did not want that to happen. But his books were already piling up around his bed and along all the corridors: they seemed to be snaking through the house with a life of their own.

"I recall that for a while, even though the situation was so desperate, Brauer spent all his time bringing his card index up to date. He was finding it increasingly hard to find the books he was looking for. People say that a book you can't find doesn't exist. But it's worse than that.

"He had an old mahogany cabinet, like the ones you used to find in offices, with a roll top and drawers where he kept his indexes, just as in public libraries. Classifying twenty thousand volumes is no easy matter. Not only do you need to have a strict respect for order—an almost superhuman respect, I would say—but you need a method and time to devote to the thankless task of cataloging works whose meaning is very different from the numbers you use to identify them. If you want to go to Amazon, for example, you have to consider a whole lot of details that will not be part of the final number, but which can lead you to it, or will be useful. If you want to write a poem, you need a piece of paper and a writing implement that works. If you want a woman to fall in love with you, you have to be prepared in all sorts of ways, some of them unpleasant, such as having to cut your toenails. When you own a library like Brauer's, you can't escape having an index. A man may conquer many books, but then a conqueror finds he has to administer them.

"Brauer didn't like the idea: he was far too keen on devouring one book after another. He had fallen behind with his index, fatally so, I think. I never believed he could finish updating it, but a few months later he told me he had almost done it. 'The worst thing,' he declared, 'the most demanding, is the question of affinities.'

"This was the first sign that something was not right. One afternoon, sitting exactly where you are now, he told me how hard it was to avoid putting two authors who had quarreled on the same shelf. For example, it was unthinkable to put a book by Borges next to one by García Lorca, whom the Argentine author once described as a 'professional Andalusian.' And given the dreadful accusations of plagiarism between the two of them, he could not put something by Shakespeare next to a work by Marlowe, even though this meant not respecting the volume numbers of the sets in his collections. Nor, of course, could he place a book by Martin Amis next to one by Julian Barnes after the two friends had fallen out, or leave Vargas Llosa with García Márquez.

"As I said, sadly, I ignored the signs that my friend was losing touch with reality. He explained that he was working on a system of decimal numbers that would be sufficiently flexible to allow him to change the position of books according to certain dynamic considerations—never speculative ones, he insisted—because when it came down to it there was nothing more fickle than literary opinion. So that if he discovered there were convincing reasons to rescue a work from oblivion, or if it achieved a new affinity with other texts, he could change its position on his shelves. So passionate was his defense of destroying his thematic index that he managed to hoodwink me for several days.

"It was one thing to be able to find books, but something very different to place them together or apart. Brauer continued to insist that kindred books should be grouped together according to criteria other than a vulgar thematic one.

"'For centuries we have used an unimaginative system,' he said, 'that refuses to recognize real affinities. I mean that *Pedro Paramo* and *Rayuela* are both written by Latin American authors, but one of them leads us back to William Faulkner, the other to Moebius. Or to put it another way: Dostoyevsky ended up closer to Roberto Arlt than he did to Tolstoy. And again: Hegel, Victor Hugo, and Sarmiento deserve to be closer together than Paco Espínola, Benedetti, and Felisberto Hernández.'

"I never managed to see in practice exactly what Carlos's classification system was like, because I had to go to the hospital for an operation and did not meet him again for several months. However, mutual friends told me he was still working on his index, was spending a lot of time studying higher mathematics, and, to the amazement of most of them, was showing signs not only of exhaustion but of madness."

Delgado stood up and walked out of the room. He came back carrying a photograph that showed a man of around fifty seated at a round table piled high with books, his back to a brick wall covered in a creeper. The bright sunlight revealed a face with well-defined features and piercing eyes, unruly hair swept back. He was in shirtsleeves, his legs were crossed, and I was surprised at how unrefined he looked.

"I took it in his back patio," Delgado said after a moment.

"He didn't wear glasses," I commented.

"He was blessed with good sight. But look for any sign of what I'm about to tell you, and you won't find it."

"One evening a friend discovered him dining opposite a magnificent edition of *Don Quixote* on a

lectern, with a glass of white wine. I don't mean the one Brauer had in his hand, but the one that was strangely placed next to the book.

"Another friend made an even odder discovery. He had to go upstairs to use the toilet because the one downstairs was out of order, and as he passed the open bedroom door, on the bed he glimpsed twenty or so books carefully laid out in such a way that they reproduced the mass and outline of a human body. He swears he could see the head, surrounded by small red-backed books, the body, the shape of arms and legs. A woman? A man? His double? We talked about it. No one could be sure, or decide what it meant. We didn't even know whether the titles had been specially chosen, although the friend thought he had recognized a volume by the Conde de Siruela; the head he thought contained the Brevarios del Fondo de Cultura Económica; the legs seemed to be several Losada editions.

"We had no notion what those books were doing on the bed, or what Brauer was doing with them. Nobody dared ask him, because the display had been installed in the intimacy of his bedroom. To me, though, it was plain that the idea of affinities had gone too far, had got out of control."

"Did anyone else see them?"

"Only that one friend," Delgado said. "He mentioned it very discreetly. We were all dumbfounded. What was an intelligent man like Brauer doing with his books now? Was he playing with them like a young girl with her dolls? Had he arranged them after thinking long and hard about their meaning? Was he trying to conjure up a figure out of paper and ink? I've no idea. But the last straw came with an accident he never forgave himself for, and to which I was a casual observer.

"I had heard that for the past two months Carlos enjoyed reading nineteenth-century French authors by candlelight, in this case provided by a silver candelabra. We had talked about it in the past, because I also like to read Goethe with a Wagner opera on my stereo, or, for example, to have Debussy accompany Baudelaire. It's part of the journey, and I can assure you it heightens one's pleasure in every sense. Perhaps you are aware that when we read under our breath, we produce the sound of the letters at an inaudible frequency. But the sound is still there. The voice is present, it is never missing. It follows the line just as an instrument follows a sheet of music, and I can assure you it's just as essential as the eyes. It creates a tone, a melody that flows through words and phrases, so that if you add real music at a soft volume, deep inside the ear a harmonic counterpoint is created between one's own voice and the music from the speakers. If the volume is too high, the music covers the voice, and the text's melody is lost. And not just that, one becomes confused. Accompanied by a good concert, poor prose can seem much better than it is.

"We joked about adding candlelight to our readings for books written before the invention of electric light. That may seem eccentric and unnecessary to you, but just try illuminating an oil painting with candlelight and you'll see it takes on a whole new aspect, however well lit it may normally be. It becomes a new painting: the shadows come to life, the flame does its work, and it is as though there were no real difference between the light coming from the pigments and oil and the room the work is in. The spaces are immersed in the same light, and you enter into another dimension.

"A similar thing occurs with some books, because a printed page is also a complicated drawing. It's a play of lines and tiny figures that flows from vowel to consonant, obeying its own laws of rhythm and composition, all based on the type size, the chosen font, the depth of the margins, the thickness of the paper, folios on the right or in the center, the infinite tiny details that go to create a beautiful object. However new the edition may be, and however white the paper, candlelight lends a book an extra luster that brings out values and subtleties in a magical way. And the pathways become a delight."

"What pathways?" I asked, unsure I had heard him right.

"Well, that's an age-old discussion. Nobody can be really sure whether it's the author's genius or the skill of the printer. Opinions are divided. But for many readers it's enough for them to look at the pathways to know whether a book is good and should be read."

Delgado went over to one of his bookcases, took out an antique edition of *Eugénie Grandet,* and handed it to me. He told me to open it at any page and to look for vertical or diagonal channels created by the spaces between words. And it was true, I could see long pathways that led from line to line, crossed paragraphs, occasionally came to a halt, then branched off diagonally, from right to left or left to right, or cascaded vertically down.

"A writer who has no rhythm to his sentences cannot create that. If he mangles the language by putting two or three words with more than four syllables in a single sentence, he is bound to block the pathway and destroy the rhythm. You look for the white spaces on the page, but you cannot find them. A clumsy edition that uses too small or too big a type size will also distort these figures that the eye feasts on in secret.

"Brauer was of the opinion that this phenomenon alone could decide an author's worth, the value of his style. I'm not so sure."

Intrigued, I handed him back the book. It was true, the pathways appeared on page after page, and they did form strange shapes.

"You mentioned an accident," I reminded him.

"Yes. Just as I was getting back into circulation, I heard not only that Carlos was reading by candlelight but that he was encouraging everyone else to do so. Never with a twentieth-century writer, of course—for them he switched on the electric light and changed the music. But he was a great lover of the nineteenth-century novel, and had a lot of records that could accompany it.

"One night he had a little too much to drink— another boon companion, though a dangerous one—and left the candelabra on top of his card index. One of the candles must have toppled over, because he awoke almost overcome by fumes and could see flames coming from the living room. It was lucky that he slept upstairs, because, as you know, smoke rises.

"The next afternoon I found him sitting by the burned index-file cabinet. He had not even come to the door to greet me. There were pools of water all over the floor; he looked as though he had not slept a wink, and was tremendously upset.

"Thankfully, his bookcases had not caught fire, which would have been a disaster. But he had lost his index, part of it burned, part of it ruined by the water. He shouted for me to come in, and as I said, he was sitting slumped in a chair staring at the black fire marks on his index cabinet. He had lost all possibility of finding most of his books, of even knowing on which shelf they might be if he could not remember exactly where he had put them. It was a tragedy for him, and I sat in silence, occasionally trying to cheer him up, though he refused to be consoled. He sat there with his hands between his knees, his hair flopping down either side of his face, his eyes staring blindly at the foot of the cabinet. I wasn't going to ask him to be polite at a time like that. So I sat with him for a while and then left, truly grieving, because to a book lover any thought of fire is like a dream turning to ashes. It's something we are constantly afraid of, a real threat, which can destroy us forever. We learn not even to mention it, hoping this may prevent its occurrence."

"What did he do then?" I hastened to ask.

"Well, before I come to that, I think it's time for you to tell me why we are talking about Carlos Brauer. If you don't mind, that is," Delgado added, in a dry tone I immediately understood. His patience was wearing thin, and he was beginning to feel used.

"I came to give him back a book he sent to a colleague who died before she could receive it."

"What was her name?" he asked, curious.

"Bluma Lennon. She worked in the Hispanic Studies Department at the University of Cambridge. She died recently—after being knocked down by a car."

Delgado looked at me in surprise, and I could see him shifting in his seat, as if Bluma's name had unsettled him.

"And please," he said, still uncertain, "could you

tell me one other thing? Was she by any chance carrying a book at the time?"

It was my turn to be taken by surprise. Where did that impossible question come from? I nodded in silence, while the figure of Delgado became suddenly hazy, as though he no longer fitted in with the idea I had formed of where I was, what he had been talking about all this time, and the eccentricities of a man devoted to journeying through his books. But my gesture unnerved him as well, and he hesitated once again. A disturbing thought struggled to surface through his body.

"One more thing. Believe me, I'm almost afraid to ask. Was the book, by any chance, by Emily Dickinson?"

I nodded again, by this time feeling very uncomfortable.

He laughed, trailing off in a hiccup. Then he fell stubbornly silent. I still had no idea what was going on.

"Don't be scared. Or perhaps both of us should be scared. I can hardly believe it!"

"Nor can I!" I said, anxious for an explanation.

"Are you sure you want to know? After the fire, Carlos finally sold his house, gave his ex-wife the money she was demanding, and traveled to Mexico. He was away three or perhaps four weeks. He wasn't well. I'll tell you about that later if you wish. But what you are waiting to hear is that when he returned from that trip, we met one Saturday at the Tristán Narvaja book market and struck up a conversation. He told me he had been on the Gulf of Mexico and in Michoacán, and among other extraordinary places he recalled, he said he had been at a writers' congress in Monterrey. 'How was it? Any good?' I asked him. Guess what he replied: 'Not bad,' he said. 'The best thing was I met a very pretty English academic. One of those feisty, confident women who are always using literary quotations and who, if they are to die, would prefer to be knocked down by a car while reading Emily Dickinson.'"

I could not contain a nervous laugh. For a few minutes we stared at each other in disbelief, as if we were part of a fable and reality had unexpectedly crumpled in front of us. Delgado stood up, went over to the small bar, and came back with a bottle of whiskey, an ice bucket, and two glasses. "The only way to take it in," he said.

While he was pouring the whiskey, I remembered Bluma's dedication in the front of the book. Something or someone had had the last laugh over the taunt that marked the end of their adventure. Carlos Brauer may not have been able to surprise her, but for the moment at least he had proved he was a better magician than Bluma. What was astonishing was not so much that despite all her efforts to demonstrate her intelligence, she had been so predictable, it was that chance or fate had responded.

However, I still had no idea what had happened to Brauer and why I could not get in touch with him.

"What did he do next?"

"The house was sold," Delgado eventually said again, his voice enlivened by the drink, although his tone was far from celebratory. "Like everyone else, I was expecting him to stay in Montevideo, but shortly after he got back from Mexico he stopped answering his doorbell—I think he disconnected it—and would not respond to telephone calls.

"Unless I'm much mistaken, that morning at Tristán Narvaja was the last time I saw him. Some time afterward, a mutual friend told me he had bought a plot of land in La Paloma with no electricity or running water, and had put up one of those shacks that has eucalyptus corner posts and a reed roof.

"It was astounding enough that such a city animal should want to live by the sea. And that's no metaphor. He built the shack right on the shore, between the lagoon at Rocha and the ocean. Do you know where I mean? There is a strip of isolated dunes whipped by the wind and threatened by high tides; on the lake side there is a cluster of poor fishermen's huts. They fish for shrimp when the sea bar opens in February, and catfish the rest of the year. You can't always reach it by car. Often you have to take a cart because the dunes shift and cover the coast road. There's another earth track higher up, but even so, to reach his hut you have to struggle across two or three hundred yards of deep sand. In other words, it's a lost place in the back of beyond. If you're not sure of the meaning of your life and want to put it to the test, or if you want to forget your thoughts and become someone else, that is the place for it. If you prefer to die of loneliness and feel like a dog, or to come face-to-face with yourself, that's the place for you. No half measures. No anesthesia. No distractions. Or consolation. A place without shade. Ruthless. With skies you're unlikely to find anywhere else. As immense at night as during the day. Oppressive. Skies to make you feel only a millimeter bigger than an insect scurrying away across the sand. I have no idea what Carlos intended to do there. But it was plain he wasn't well, or at the very least, that losing his index in the fire had ended all his hopes of classifying his library.

"That is no small thing. I hope you understand. Just imagine for a moment that over your lifetime you've stored up memories of your childhood: sensations, smells, the light shining on your mother's

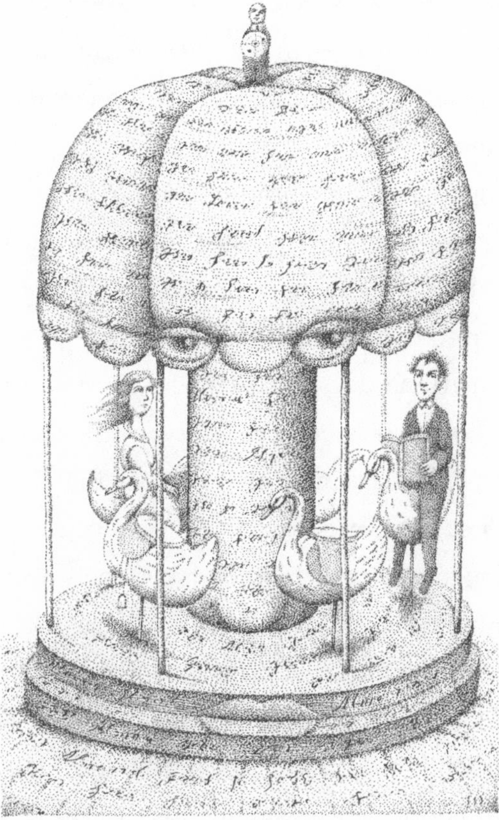

hair, your first adventures on your street, the impressions of things that may be unfathomable and chaotic but which when put together constitute the memory of your childhood, with its terrors, joys, and emotions. After that, you have a checklist of growing up. School brings order. Your teachers, classmates, the first romantic adventures: you go on accumulating memories of all your experiences right up to the present.

"Then one day, unexpectedly, you lose the sequence of these memories. They're still there, but you can't find them. You search for the image of your first wife, and you find the shoe a dog was chewing in a distant childhood wasteland. You look for your mother's face, and come up with that of an unpleasant character in some gloomy municipal office. Your personal history is lost. I thought about all this while I was trying to understand what Carlos did. The worst thing about it is that the facts are there, just waiting for someone to stumble on them. But you don't have the key. It's not forgetfulness drawing its kind veil over things we cannot tolerate.

It's a sealed memory, an obsessive call to which there is no answer. He doesn't even have the thematic index that he rejected in favor of his new, more complex system, which turned out to be far too fragile.

"But he did take his books to Rocha with him. To the strip of sand between the lagoon and sea. It was an expensive move, because the books had to travel more than two hundred kilometers in covered trucks. They had to go in along the earth road and then be taken across the dunes by cart, until, finally, they arrived at the lean-to shack almost on the beach.

"Then what do you think he did with them? He set about finding a local out-of-work laborer, one of those men who are as competent working with wood as they are with cement, who can put in a window or thatch a roof, hammer in nails as big as your finger, drill for water or chisel stone, although you can never be sure of the results. The kind of man who asks no questions but follows instructions, whatever they may be, providing he gets paid, because he won't have to live there.

"Brauer told his laborer to build the supports for the windows and two doors on the sand. He got him to build a stone wall, and a chimney. Once the chimney was built at the side of the shack, and the door and window frames completed, he asked him to put in a cement floor. And on that floor—you can imagine the horror that fills me as I say this— he told him to turn his books into bricks.

"Yes, that's right. The laborer looked on with a mixture of pity and indifference as he began to choose from the mountain of books the cart had tipped onto the clean white sand, those he wanted to protect him from the wind, the rain, the rigors of winter. He had long since forgotten any idea of friendship or enmity between authors, the affinities or contradictions between Spinoza, the botany of the Amazon, and Virgil's *Aeneid*; or any concern for fine or mediocre bindings, whether they had engravings or plates, were uncut or even incunables. All he was worried about was their size, their thickness, how resistant their covers might be to lime, cement and sand. The laborer squared off one of the volumes of an encyclopedia in the corner angle, then used a string to line the others up to make a straight wall.

"I have no trouble imagining him saying: 'Why not? They are irregular like stone. They're more regular than stone in fact. They're almost bricks. Don't worry. This is easy.'

"I can see Carlos sitting, hands on his lap, in a chair between the huge pile of books the cart had left and the shoreline, wearing a straw hat to protect him from the fierce Rocha sun, listening to the sound of the laborer's trowel on the backs of books whose margins he had scrawled on with useless references to other works, commentaries he could never again check, consult, or cast light on with a further reading. He is neither happy nor sad, more dumbstruck by his own brutal act, and lulled by the laborer's whistle, the radio playing, or the ocean waves breaking on the shore, the gulls on the beach.

"I've thought a lot about it. As the walls were going up, he must have walked around, handing the laborer a Borges to fit in under the windowsill, a Vallejo for the door, with Kafka above it and Kant beside it, plus a hardback edition of Hemingway's *A Farewell to Arms*; Cortázar and Vargas Llosa, who always writes thick books; Valle Inclán next to Aristotle, Camus with Morosoli; Shakespeare fatally bound to Marlowe by the mortar of cement; and all of them destined to raise a wall, to cast a shadow. 'It'll keep you warm, I reckon,' the laborer would shout to encourage him, to help him relax his fixed stare, as set as if he too had fallen into a bucket of mortar. Because his face took on the lonely destiny of those books, which nobody would ever open again, or look at avidly, or give him the opportunity to say to an admiring visitor: 'Actually, no, I haven't read them all. They've kept me company for many years. Look, here's something I'm sure will amaze you.'

"But he could say: they are still my friends. They give me shelter. Shade in the summer. They shield me from the winds. The books are my house. Nobody could deny him that, even though the outcome was a bleak one, and such close companionship with the most delicate aspect of books had ended up with him being cast on this remote, secluded beach.

"In a week the laborer raised, page by page, volume by volume, edition by edition, the walls of this hut on the sands of Rocha; Carlos Brauer's life's work disappeared under the cement. One work destroyed inside another. Not just sealed up. Demolished in cement.

"I heard he lived there for a while, and that the cardboard, pasteboard, and paper, bound and welded into the mortar, proved more resistant than anyone could have imagined. Of course, they could not bear the weight of the roof, but the four corner posts did that. They did support their own weight, stay intact, and keep out the weather. Maybe you've seen how cement blocks crumble, how bricks can split. But the bookbindings were stronger."

Delgado fell silent, and I was so astounded by what he had said I did not want to disturb him. It was obvious he felt overwhelmed by a story he found painful to recall.

"I think the book he sent Bluma must have come from there," I eventually managed to say.

He looked at me in astonishment. His face twisted in a sad air of refusal that alarmed me.

"Don't tell me anything. I don't want to know."

His blue eyes narrowed. He glanced down at his watch and asked me to leave. He promised he would see me again the next day, but told me to give him a call to confirm the appointment.

I was afraid he would not keep it.

four

Over the years I have seen books used to prop up a table, known them make a bedside table, piled up one above the other with a cloth over the top; many dictionaries have ironed and pressed things more often than they have been opened; and more than one book has kept letters, money, and secrets hidden on their shelves. People can also change the destiny of books.

A vase, coffeepot, or TV gets broken much more easily than a book. A book does not come apart unless its owner wants it to, tears out its pages, burns them. In the years of the last military dictatorship in Argentina, a lot of people burned books in their lavatories and baths, or buried them at the bottom of their garden. Books had become extremely dangerous. Having to choose between them and life itself, Argentines became their own executioners.

Books that had been closely studied and debated, books that had roused passions and resolute commitments or distanced old friends, rose to the heavens as ashes that vanished in the air.

I could not bring myself to do it. I rolled up magazines and stuffed them into the bathroon curtain pole, hid the most notorious books at the back of wardrobes or in the most remote of my bookshelves, even though I knew a sudden raid would mean they might be uncovered. In those days books accused many people. They ruined their lives.

The relations humanity has had with these tough objects capable of surviving one, two, or twenty centuries, of in some way defeating the sands of time, have never been innocent. A human vocation has become attached to this soft, indestructible wood pulp.

I'm not one for looking under chairs. I like to

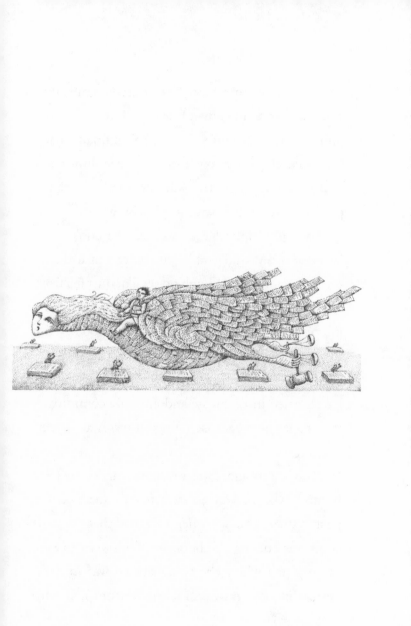

be taken in by puppeteers, the theater's simple illusions and the melody of words. But the paper house on that distant southern beach finally made me aware of the shadow line: an unseen dimension that brings together the will and the body of the printed letter in this strange plaything.

Back in Cambridge, I returned the book to its lectern on my study table, and Alice put a duster under it again, even though no cement dust fell from it any longer. I had a month to prepare myself for the interview for Bluma's job, and this was a good excuse to forget the book's silent, challenging presence.

I could not bring myself to tell anybody what I had learned in Uruguay, and am only committing it to paper now because I am still trying to understand it.

Two nights ago, I was reading an article by John Bernon, who had taken over from Laurel on the postgraduate courses, when I realized that the table lamp was cutting the book on the lectern in two: the top half where the title featured was in darkness, while the gray, crumbling bottom half with the colophon was lit up. I found it impossible to go on reading, to ignore its call. Chance and curiosity were my part of the story, but that volume which had crossed hemispheres four times already was part of a destiny.

I got up from my seat, put the book in an envelope, and shut it in a drawer.

Yesterday afternoon I visited Bluma's grave. We had buried her in a charming but crowded green cemetery on the city outskirts. As I was driving there through a drizzle, I felt I was a messenger bringing a futile warning. The smear of rain on my windscreen reminded me of Carlos Brauer's house on the Uruguayan coast, between lagoon and ocean, one afternoon of heavy, vertical clouds, so huge and menacing that each one of them seemed like a storm in itself. As I had suspected, Delgado avoided meeting me again. I called him at home several times, left messages on his answering machine, even tried to get in touch with him at the Chamber of Commerce, where I could not get beyond the friendly obstacle of his secretary. I found his attitude objectionable and yet comprehensible. This sybarite of books could not go on with Brauer's story without a profound sense of horror. But my holiday period was almost at an end, and I was desperate to see with my own eyes the place from where *The Shadow-Line* had departed.

Less prepared than I should have been, I had taken a bus to La Paloma. It was the end of June, and the empty, silent town, its shops boarded up as if the cruel southern winter had forced them to protect themselves, greeted me at midday with winds from the sea that whipped at the palm trees lining its streets. Several pine trunks had been knocked down across the road into town, but still not satisfied, the wind tore at their flailing branches.

It was not the best day to visit the resort, but it was my only free day and my last chance. By some miracle or other I managed to find a taxi driver willing to take me to the lagoon. As Delgado had said, to do this we had to go back to the main highway and make a lengthy detour along a dirt track full of potholes, like a dried-up riverbed. The driver confirmed that the coast road was blocked.

I had no trouble identifying the spot. We rounded a bend, and then the road led straight between the lake and the sand dunes. In the distance I soon saw the solitary hut. On the land side, beyond an arm of the lake, I could see the hills of a country estate, then the land dipped again, and there was only an immense stretch of water disappearing to the horizon. The winter tides had flooded a row of corrugated iron and board huts. A few horses, dogs, and fishermen were splashing about in the water, in among hanging nets and boats rocked by the current. Some of the men looked up in surprise when they saw the taxi coming, then returned to their tasks with that alert reticence I had come to recognize from the previous days.

Asking the taxi driver to wait, I reached the hut wearing a handkerchief round my face to ward off the stinging sand. I could make out the rough gray expanse of the graceful, pitching ocean; I could see thick flecks of iodine spilling onto the shore, gathering into great clumps, and pushing up the beach in a thick grimy line of foam, while the wind tore off great chunks and sent them flying along with sand, bits of plastic and small pieces of driftwood; on the beach I could sea a few gulls, perched on the corpses of huge seals. The wind and rain had reduced the hut itself to a skeleton, with the wooden frames still intact but all the rest a pile of rubble. Nothing Bluma could have imagined on the streets of Monterrey or between the sheets of her hotel bed, in the poems of Emily Dickinson or any other book she had read with less drastic consequences. What remained of the walls were bowed, jagged fragments, and in among the clumps of cement, tiny seashells, and dark lichens, I could make out pages of books baked in the sun then soaked, glued together like cuttlefish beaks, the type bleached and illegible; the cover of an encyclopedia, the swollen white froth of a paperback with its wavy, twisted edges.

Half-hidden in the sand around the doors and windows, I found copies of Huidobro, Neruda, and Bartolomé de las Casas; then a solid brick of

Lawrence and Marosa di Giorgio, bits of Eliot and Lorca, Burckhardt's *Renaissance* encrusted with barnacles, an unrecognizable Pallière covered in tar.

"Twenty thousand dollars!" I shouted, turning my back to the wind, which had loosened one of the roof beams and was banging it against a corner post. There the books were, buried in stone, torn, shrouded in a black coating of dirt I could not scrape off. Impossible to get at them without some kind of implement. All I could do was plunge my hands down until I felt a solid shape. When I pulled it to the surface, there was only a grotesque mess. Each volume appeared on the sand like a sinister cadaver. Paper and words, washed out ink, covers drilled by insects that had dug hundreds of small idiosyncratic tunnels between pages and chapters.

Kneeling there with the handkerchief still covering my face, for a moment I imagined I might find a first edition of Arlt or Darío in perfect condition, the volume of *Don Quixote* that shared a drink with Brauer, but all I pulled out were improbable bricks containing the bones of a García Márquez, a sticky pulp that had been a Lope de Vega, or the taut skin of Balzac.

All of a sudden I stopped digging and stood up, overcome by a sense of terror and anguish. Universal literature was poking up out of the sand with a demeaning summons. The books were there, they were still there, bound and baked, their pages riddled with broader pathways than those any genius could produce, under those splitting crusts through which part of a cover suddenly appeared like an eye, spines pushing up to the light only to fall back into their tomb of sand.

I left the books on the dunes and walked toward the shack. The doors and windows had been torn off, but their skeletons offered disconsolate views of the landscape beyond, with no other background than the unhinged rectangles of their frames. The wind whistled a mournful tune in the reeds of what remained of the roof.

The stone chimney still stood proud, and the cement floor was still visible in fragments free of sand. I was tempted to take out my copy of *The*

Shadow-Line and leave it by a corner of the hearth together with the other corpses of a voyage that the beach was consuming day by day, because even in the heady, tenacious hope of the printed word, made possible by printers, designers, secretaries, typesetters, commentators, writers, and messengers, craftsmen in inks and bindings, illustrators, prologue writers, cultured critics of memory, paper is an organic product that, like the pine trees on the road, sooner or later falls prey to the jaws of the sea in a silent, devastating collapse.

And there was the sea, turbulent and eager, each wave like a snap of jaws, and there were the seals with their bloody rib cages exposed to the albatrosses' hungry beaks. And the iodine in the air, the gusts of sand, great tree trunks thrown up on the shore at the end of their incredible journey. What else could a book do here but bury itself in the sand, let itself be eaten away in the darkness, suddenly break the surface like the remains of a shipwreck?

But I could not bring myself to leave the book there. I held on to it so as not to give in to lack of

faith and disgust, because even if this is our common destiny—the book's, mine, and that of everything that one day crawled out of the ocean's ghastly slime to invent a meaning for itself on land, it could be resisted, and even if all we can do is offer a slow, prolonged delay, then it will be for others finally to surrender the word to its fate.

So I brought the book back like a talisman, and clung on to it with all the terrified faith I could muster. For several weeks I celebrated its vagabond presence on my study table; together, we laughed at the stuffy volumes on my bookshelves, absurdly reproaching them for having no more idea of life than a spotless shelf, the tickle of a feather duster, the vacuum cleaner removing all their dust, asleep and only occasionally waking to their task, with a pride never threatened by the violence or forces of nature outlined in their pages.

But my euphoria gradually subsided. Haunted by the ghost of Brauer, I made a thorough clear-out and put all the books I judged inessential or not directly useful in big cardboard boxes. I gave several of them to my students or colleagues, glad to have reclaimed spaces where I could hang a painting or a mirror, a smooth white surface that made no call on my attention.

At night, though, I was having nightmares. I found myself on the dunes again, where it was not books but hands that poked up through the sand, grabbing my ankles to prevent me escaping their desperate plea.

Preparing for my interview slowly drove these images from my mind. I had to compete against three well-qualified lecturers, but finally I was chosen to replace Bluma, even though by now I was not sure I wanted to. Sometimes I felt an overwhelming urge to become a sailor in Alaska, to change course entirely, to go back to Buenos Aires and forget books. But then I told myself I was still being affected by Brauer's story, and should not allow myself to be carried away by its spell. I wondered where he could be, if he was happy without any books, if he had gone into business or if little by little, without meaning to, he had set out to build another library.

However intriguing his destiny might be, I had to continue with my own, keep on course with the goal I had set myself: to trace a map of Latin American literature on its passage through Europe, thus completing in some way or other Bluma's outward journey. My problem was that ever since my experience in Uruguay, this ambition seemed pretentious when compared with the journey books themselves make. This had become my discovery and my undoing.

I considered books in bookshop windows, glittering in the spotlights like great colored gems, and although I still read their titles, I could not suppress a cynical, unpleasant desire to consider their size and volume as well. What would become of all their charm, this wonderful display of covers and bindings, if fate were to get its teeth into them as well, showed them what wind, fire, and water can do?

Within a few days I was looking apprehensively at new books, and resisting all temptation at the bargain tables. Worse still, almost without a second thought, I consigned to the library vaults all the copies of books that arrived from far-off countries. I was terrified that one of them might interest me and I would find myself taking it home and so make further additions to the gigantic colony that had established itself on my walls and was taking over the corridors.

And if I placed *The Shadow-Line* back on the lectern where I could see it every day, this was because I doubted whether I was strong enough to avoid breaking my promise to myself. Then came the night when I saw it cut in half by the lamplight, and whether because Brauer was right to suggest that books create their own affinities or because I had finally come to my senses, I decided it was time to visit Bluma's grave.

I placed the book on the passenger seat, and drove on. The steadily increasing rain forced me to switch on my headlights and to try to recall my unlikely point of departure. I stopped at a pub to buy cigarettes, and when I got back to the car I sat for a quarter of an hour under an ash tree listening to the monotonous swish of the windscreen wipers sweeping off the rain. Was I being fair to Joseph? Did Conrad have to bite the dust as well?

"And again he pleaded for the promise that I would not leave him behind. I had the firmness of mind not to give it to him. Afterward this sternness seemed criminal; for my mind was made up," the captain said of the delirious sailor on his sickbed, victim of a "downright panic." In those words it seemed to me I heard the tacit appeal the book had been making to me from the very start.

I put the car in gear and drove back to the main road. A few miles farther on I turned into the long avenue of trees leading to the cemetery. There I parked by an elm tree and walked, book in hand, between the rows of graves with their little patch of garden, graves that themselves looked like sealed books, so oblong and stiff that no one could ever open them, each with their own story of a will to live couched in the damp earth.

The gentle rain had succeeded in heightening the green of the foliage and the headstones. I had trouble finding the spot where Bluma's remains lay.

I pulled up my coat collar to keep out the rain while an attendant led me to the grave she was allotted. I placed the book in the solitary, silent center of the marble slab.

I stood before it for a moment, as the raindrops fell onto the rough cover, as intact in the rain as it had been when it endured the cement and its voyage of return. Without realizing it, the Rocha fishermen had told me the end of the story.

"Too much space for someone not used to it," one of the two men had said when they began the tale, as we sat in their flooded shack, the water halfway up our legs.

Just as I had been about to climb back into the taxi, I decided on impulse to go over to the fishermen's houses, telling myself I would not have another opportunity to find out what they knew. From the track I clapped my hands, and the dogs came toward me and the horses shied away. A few seconds later the two men appeared from behind a wall, and when I asked for the owner of the house they waved and shouted for me to approach. That was no easy matter. A few steps farther on, the dark line of floodwater from the lagoon began, and I had no idea how deep it was. Their invitation was so insistent, however, that I took off my shoes and socks, rolled my trousers up and advanced timidly and hesitantly about a hundred yards until I reached the hut, shoes in hand.

To my surprise, they seemed so calmly resigned to living submerged in water that had it not been for the cold in my calves I too would have managed to ignore it. They had laid their mattresses on tall tables; another table was piled high with tools, crockery, and a small gas stove; the rest of their wretched belongings hung from hooks on the walls. The open door looked out onto the lagoon, which extended to a horizon of heavy black clouds, while the fishermen's boats swayed at anchor only a few yards from the hut, and in the water behind them clustered flocks of ducks, gulls, and flamingoes.

The two fishermen told me they had grown accustomed to living with the man. They used to see him strolling on the beach or round the lagoon, or setting off on long walks from which he returned several hours later with armfuls of driftwood, seal bones, flotsam, colored bottles. He had used the wood to make some bits of furniture and shelves, and hung the bones on fishing lines inside and outside the hut, together with the skeletons of albatrosses and other birds. On windy days they banged into each other with such a clatter they could not imagine how he managed to sleep, or why he had hung them up in the first place. This led everyone to keep away from the hut, and the women forbade their children to go near.

Just once, an old woman had gone to ask him to take the evil eye from her that had given her such a swollen belly it was on the point of bursting. She came back disappointed, claiming he was a sorcerer with no powers except perhaps to cause "harm," so after that everyone kept away.

Sometimes they would see him reading one of the books that had apparently been left over, protected from the sun by his roof. In summer he

would go to La Paloma and have food delivered to him; in winter he went to a store run by a fisherman to buy rum, loose tobacco, the odd bag of flour, pasta, whatever he needed to keep going. He didn't say much, and the fishermen didn't "chat" with him more than necessary. Nobody knew what he did. Or what he was searching for.

A summer, a winter, and another summer went by in this way. In August, when the whales were heading south, they said that several of them had paused level with the hut, flapped their enormous fins, and called and splashed far more than was usual; this made a great impression on the fishing community. A baby whale got stuck on a sandbank a few yards from the shore, and ten men waded into the water to free it. This took some time, but Brauer did not come near them; he simply watched from his hut, with the bones clinking around him, lonely and unmoved, until the creature was back in the water.

Then one morning a few months ago, they said, they had seen him taking a hammer to the hut walls. What most impressed them was that he did not appear to be trying to fix anything, because he would hammer at one end, and then start again at the other. They would see him at work above a window, then below it, then by a door. One of their neighbor's kids, the only one who dared talk "to the gentleman," came back with an explanation that removed their initial amazement, only to plunge them into a greater state of confusion: "he was looking for a book" the boy told them.

They knew the bricks in the hut were not all cement, and for a long time they had bet on how long walls like that would last. The laborer had been boasting in the bars along the coast that he had built a paper house, but no one would believe him.

"But here we knew it was true, even though we hadn't actually seen it," the older, more talkative of the fishermen said. The other man, possibly his son or a relative, merely nodded and moved his hands jerkily.

"A lot of tourists come here and behave as they

see fit," the older man went on. "Well, each to his own I suppose. He had built his house from books, which was astounding enough. Even more surprising was when he started to knock holes in it. As I say, for two days he was demolishing the walls, and the kid said it was because he couldn't find the book he wanted. You've seen it: how many books could there be?

"Anyway by the end he left the house like a sieve. At least ten or more gaping holes in each wall. Top, bottom, on the side. Until at last he found it, or so the boy said. He found it and took the book to La Paloma, and sent it off by post. The boy knew, because he went with him.

"Then the man returned, and we saw him start to repair the hut. He bought a bag of cement and had a cartload of stones delivered. But what can I say? Nothing seemed to work. First it collapsed on one side, then the other. He would line up a book, but the wall underneath would buckle and seem to be about to collapse. And the books high up in the walls? They all fell down. Everything was loose and warped, it was impossible to mend. He spent days rebuilding, but have you been there? There's nothing left. In the end, he destroyed it himself. We saw him from here with his sledgehammer. We all felt sorry for him, I can tell you. Because the house wasn't bad at all, until he became obsessed with that one book.

"One afternoon we saw him on the track, carrying a suitcase. He looked back at the demolished hut, waved to us, and walked off in the baking sun. He never came back."

I was saying good-bye to the fishermen, carrying my shoes, my bare feet frozen, when it occurred to me to ask awkwardly whether in the days before his departure they had noticed anything strange. Their eyes opened wide, and the old man replied:

"Strange is what he had been from the start. Who knows what he had been doing there? As I said, nobody had much to do with him because we were all a bit scared. All except for the kid, who's a brave lad. He said the man was no sorcerer, that he read things out loud to him that he didn't really understand, but which sounded like music, and he had no idea what the bones were doing there. He asked the gentleman about them once, but he smiled a sad smile and said nothing.

"Can I talk to the boy?" I asked him.

"He's in Arachnia, working on a building site with his uncle."

"But there was a letter," the other man suddenly said. "The kid took him a letter that had arrived in La Paloma. From England," he concluded, as if that one word evoked a sense of mystery and strangeness that would accompany the story for the rest of his life.

I kept this detail in mind as I struggled across the lake up to my knees, once again in water and mud, then during the taxi ride, in the bus to Montevideo, the hydrofoil to Buenos Aires, and, after recovering from a terrible cold at my mother's, during the flight to London.

That detail was also the proof I needed as I stood by Bluma's grave yesterday afternoon, watching the rain course over the cement and seeing fragments of the old boat and fishes on the cover illustration appear from under the crust concealing them, as if, driven on by a secret desire, the ship had suddenly cast off. Because Bluma had written to ask him to send back the book she had given him in Monterrey—I found a copy of the letter on her computer the day after I got back—which she claimed was indispensable for her to complete her thesis on Conrad. This was I am sure untrue, because apart from the dedication I do not think she had written anything in it, and she would have had no difficulty buying another copy in English or Spanish in any bookshop. I suspected another reason. Perhaps simply the curiosity to see whether this remote man, with whom she had spent a single night of panting and tequilas in a Monterrey hotel, not only remembered her fondly but was capable of doing something for her.

The book was turning soft in the rain, melting into the marble stone, slipping into a slow but serene death like a boat silently entering port. Once again, I imagined Carlos Brauer with his gnawing doubts, trying to remember where exactly the book had ended up in the whitewashed wall, blindly running his hand over the rough surface in the hope that a tingling in his fingers might help him to find it, stuck to another book. For an instant I imagined him growing angry at himself, not at having forgotten, but knowing that it was there, somewhere under the cement, and becoming more determined than ever to uncover it. Had he done it for her? Or for himself, at his wits' end with loneliness, with hearing the books calling out to him beneath the clinking of the bones in the wind? Or was it all justified by the naive but imperious need of a woman demanding to be surprised, a challenge that was the final stage of something that had to reach its end, had finished long before for him, so that all he could do was pick up his sledgehammer and start to demolish his life's work yet again, in the hope of breaking out of his prison?

In the rain, the book had come too late to surprise Bluma, and she had not profited from its lesson. Yet brutally, unsteadily, but with a sure hand, a man had crossed his shadow line.

I bade Bluma farewell. As the illustration of the ship and the fishes began to dissolve, I saluted the great Joseph and turned for home.

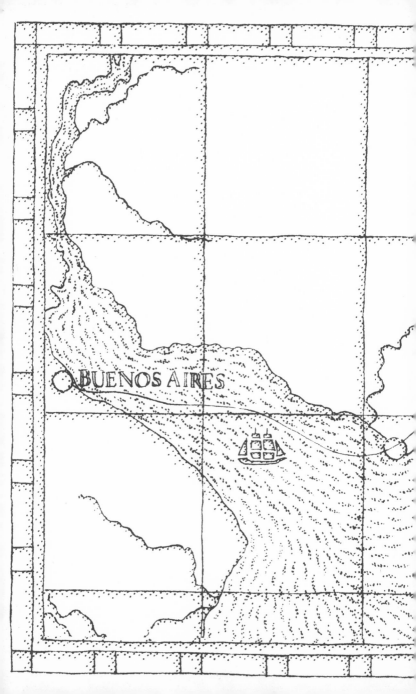